For Andy, Chris, and Mike
C. M. xxx

First American edition published in 2009 by Boxer Books Limited.

Distributed in the United States and Canada by Sterling Publishing Co., Inc.
387 Park Avenue South, New York, NY 10016-8810
First published in Great Britain in 2009 by Boxer Books Limited.

www.boxerbooks.com

Text and Illustrations copyright © 2009 Cathy MacLennan

The rights of Cathy MacLennan to be identified as the author and illustrator of this work
have been asserted by her in accordance with the Copyright, Designs and Patents Act, 1988.

The illustrations were prepared using acrylic paints on green kraft paper.
The text is set in Addled.

ISBN 13: 978-1-906250-30-0

1 3 5 7 9 10 8 6 4 2

Printed in China

All of our papers are sourced from managed forests and renewable resources.

Monkey Monkey Monkey

Cathy MacLennan

Boxer Books

Monkey swings and Monkey plays.
Monkey-monkey does!

What Monkey wants is monkey nuts!

Monkey-monkey-monkey nuts!

So Monkey looks and Monkey finds . . .

Spots, spots! Fur, fur!

Furry, furry spots.

Then leafy logs and toothy crocs,
and lots and lots of frogs!
Monkey wants some monkey nuts!
Monkey-monkey-monkey nuts!

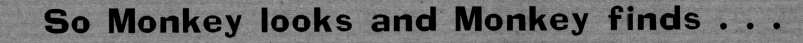

So Monkey looks and Monkey finds . . .

Tall trees and long streams—
insect, insect, insect beams!

But Monkey wants some monkey nuts!

Monkey-monkey-monkey nuts!

So Monkey climbs and Monkey finds . . .

Walking, talking leaves,

and creeping, crawling seeds.

And rainbow birds,
tu-whit, tu-whoo!
Twitters,
   twitters,
      tweets!

But Monkey wants
some monkey nuts!
Monkey-monkey-monkey nuts!
So Monkey climbs higher
and Monkey finds . . .

Fruity fruit and friendly friends,
Flowery, funny fun!
But Monkey wants
some monkey nuts!
Monkey-monkey-monkey nuts!

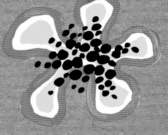

So Monkey-monkey
waves good-bye
and climbs . . .

Higher . . .

HIGHER . . .

HIGHER!

Then Monkey looks and Monkey finds
clouds and breeze and tops of trees,
a lovely, leafy canopy!

But the sky is **SO BIG**
and Monkey is so small.

Monkey-monkey wants his mommy!

Monkey-monkey holds his tummy!

Monkey-monkey's

VERY HUNGRY!

Monkey cries.
Monkey listens.
He waits to hear
his mommy's call.

Then Monkey's **DADDY** scoops him up
and takes his little monkey home!

Monkey's very quiet now,
snuggled up with Mom and Dad.

Furry, fluffy cuddles
and soft, sweet snuggles.
Then Monkey sees
and Monkey finds
down,
   down
      below . . .

A lovely, scrumptious,
tummy-load of
monkey-monkey-monkey nuts.

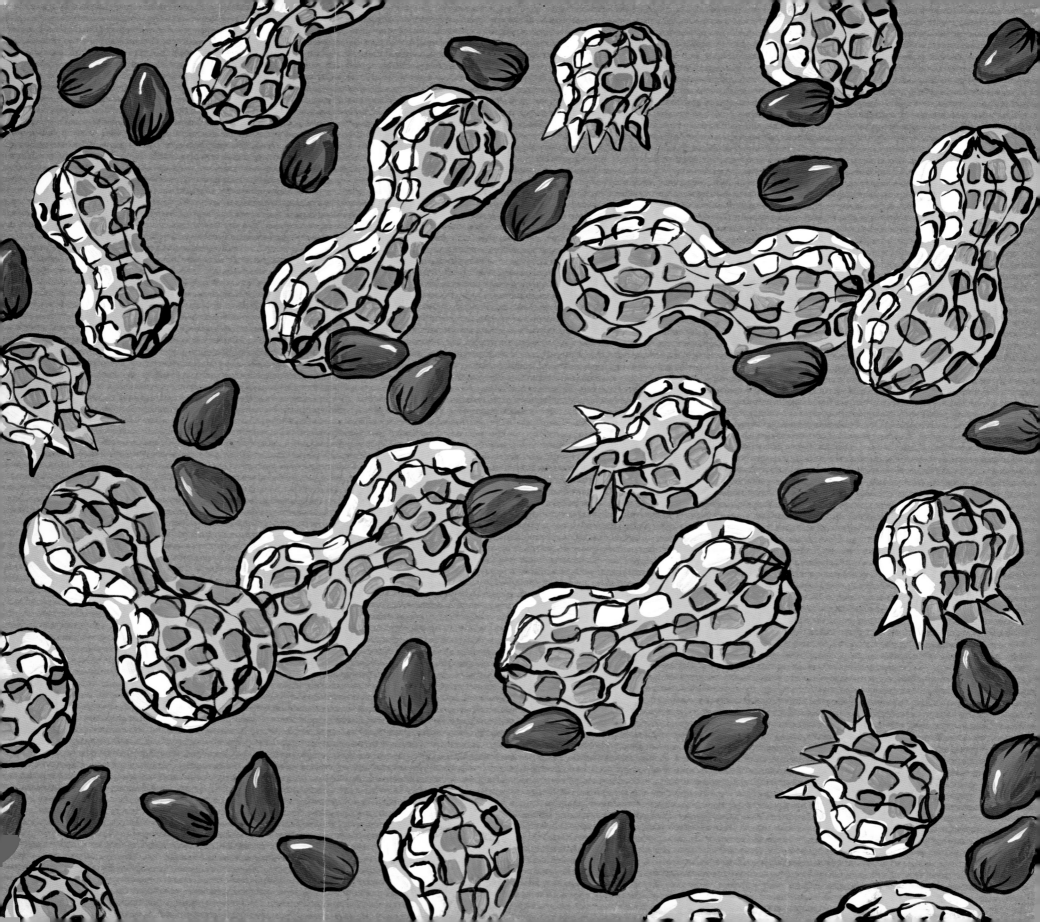